Tom and Lilly's
—Planet Munch—
Adventures

Ayati Rudrabhatla

Limited Special Edition. No. 20 of 25 Paperbacks

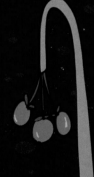

Ayati Rudrabhatla began illustrating since the age of 5 and hasn't stopped since. She was inspired to write and illustrate this book by her idols Mary Blair and Ronald Searle. She came up with the idea of the book at the age of 8 but the concept of the book clicked at the age of 12. Thus began the creation of the book.

TOM AND LILLY'S
—Planet Munch—
ADVENTURES

Ayati Rudrabhatla

AUSTIN MACAULEY PUBLISHERS™
LONDON ★ CAMBRIDGE ★ NEW YORK ★ SHARJAH

ISBN 9781528973304 (Paperback)
ISBN 9781528973328 (ePub e-book)

www.austinmacauley.com

First Published (2019)
Austin Macauley Publishers Ltd
25 Canada Square
Canary Wharf
London
E14 5LQ

Dedicated to Anya

Petra Peach

Chase Cherry

Greta Grapes

Wendy Watermelon

Ora Orange

Stella Strawberry

Riley Raspberry

Pia Pineapple

Arnold Apple

King Aubergine

Dr Carrot

Toto Tomato

Lincoln Leek

Chris Cucumber

Carol Corn

Mable Mushroom

Leman Lemon

Adal Avocado

Ola Onion

Beatrice Brocolli

Iola Ice Lolly

Mano Marshmallow

Ica Ice Cream

Bala Biscuit

Barry Burger

Pauline Pizza

Bobo Brown Bar

Cara Cupcake

Queen Candyfloss

Wes Wafer

Fiona Fizz

It was a beautiful sunny day. Tom and Lilly were having a picnic at the park.

Lilly devoured delicious treats soaked in sugar while Tom savoured his colourful fruit and vegetables.

Tom noticed that Lilly hadn't touched her vegetables at all but just relished the sickly-sweet treats.

He decided to take her on a trip to Planet Munch, to show her all the wonderful things about fruit and vegetables.

Brimming with excitement, Lilly and Tom set off to explore the spectacular Planet Munch.

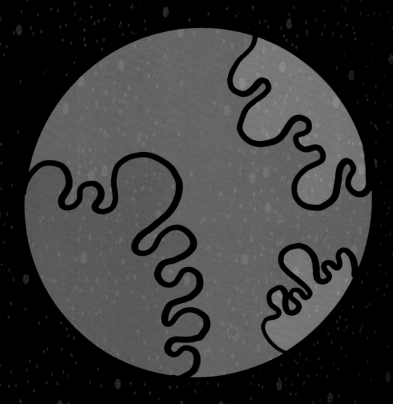

This planet was home to every food imaginable, from ruby-red raspberries to marvellous marshmallows.

They had arrived! Lilly and Tom
landed their spaceship in the
Green Kingdom.

A flurry of fruits and vegetables
bounded up the hill to explore the
spaceship.

Keen to meet the twins, King Aubergine invited Tom and Lilly to his Artichoke Palace. Lilly was surprised by the kindness of King Aubergine. She had always thought fruit and vegetables were horrible. Had she been wrong all this time?

King Aubergine lived in the Artichoke Palace. The fruit and vegetables flourished under his rule in the Green Kingdom. Sometimes, the fruit and vegetables fought battles with their foes from Fructose Fallows. King Aubergine desperately wanted to bring peace between the squabbling food kingdoms.

The glorious Green Kingdom was adorned with red cherry lamp-posts which lit up the busy streets, once the sky ripened into hues of berry-blue with glistening stars. The potato-peel pathways were full of hustle and bustle; foods from all kingdoms travelled here to dine at the popular restaurant, Roots. Lilly was now curious to see her favourite treats, so they were off to Fructose Fallows.

On arrival in Fructose Fallows, Tom and Lilly met Queen Candyfloss. The Green Kingdom had warned them about the queen.

22

She was portrayed as manipulative and mischievous. She apparently hid her spies everywhere on Earth. Supposedly, they had been camped out everywhere... Even KETCHUP!

Lilly was amazed by the bubblegum-pink mountains and the marmalade-orange streets. On arrival, an audience with the queen was demanded. "My sister and I have come to this planet so I can show her the kingdom of fruit and vegetables, but she insisted we visit you," said Tom. Outraged, the queen insisted that Fructose Fallows was the greatest and healthiest kingdom.

charge! The two kingdoms bounded towards each other with their ammunition. The sweet treats fired their candy cola guns at the valiant Green Kingdom.

In return the Greens exploded cherry bombs and catapulted their sweet pea soldiers. The fruits and vegetables fought arduously. Their vitamin and mineral powers helped them fight better and longer than the treats. The Fructose fighters tried to hold them off by blasting freezing ice rockets.

AGHHHH

The prolonging battle lasted for days. However, the kingdom that had won was...

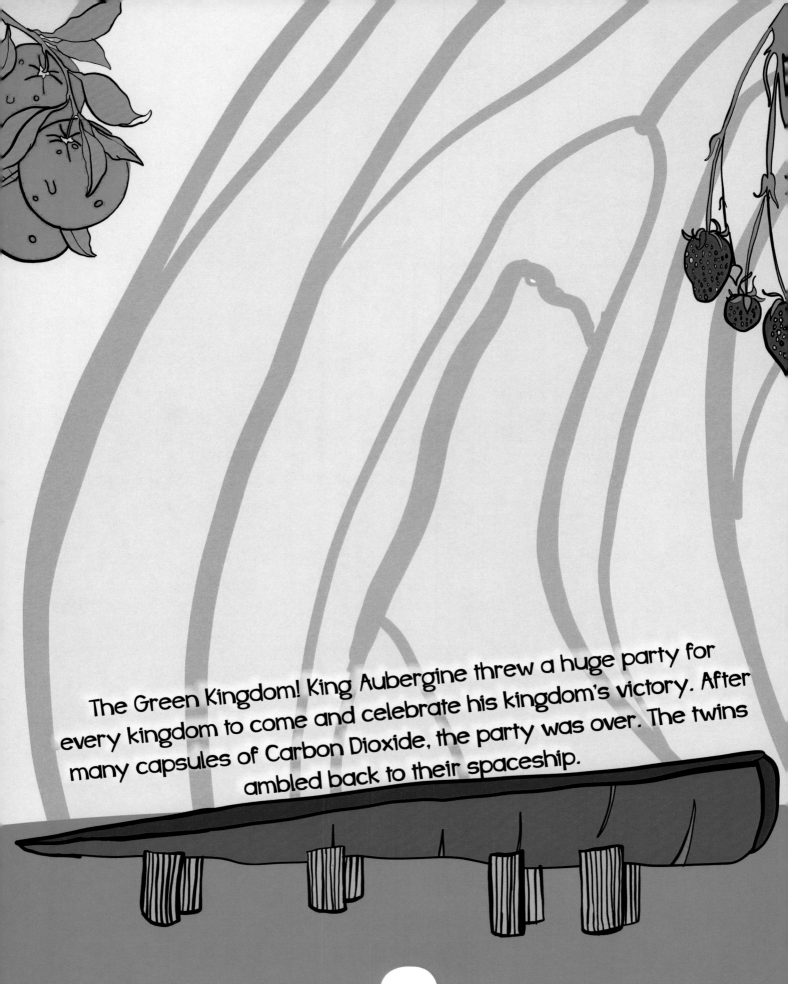

The Green Kingdom! King Aubergine threw a huge party for every kingdom to come and celebrate his kingdom's victory. After many capsules of Carbon Dioxide, the party was over. The twins ambled back to their spaceship.

Tom and Lilly soared home in their blazing-red rocket from their wondrous adventure. This trip had made Lilly realise chocolate cake is not the only delicious food out there.

Carb Kingdom

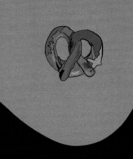

Yolk's Hostel

Pretzel Patrol
Office

Lentil Palace

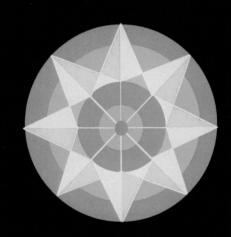

Gumball
Look-Out

Meringue
Mountains

Trifle Towers

Tart's Bakery

34

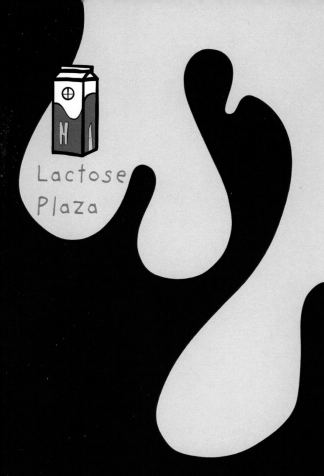

Lactose
Plaza

Cow's Cream

Cheddar
Chateau

Artichoke
Alcazar

Apple Blossom
Nursery

Look-Out
Station

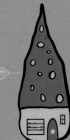

Dr Carrot's
Optician Centre